THE STRAY
CAT'S TALE

IAN STRACHAN

Illustrated by
VANESSA JULIAN-OTTIE

HEINEMANN·LONDON

William Heinemann Ltd
A division of Reed Children's Books
Michelin House
81 Fulham Road London SW3 6RB

London • Melbourne • Auckland

First published 1995
Text copyright © Ian Strachan 1995
Illustrations copyright © Vanessa Julian-Ottie 1995
ISBN 0 434 97387 4

Produced by Mandarin Offset Ltd.
Printed in China

A school pack of BANANA BOOKS 79-84 is
available from Heinemann Educational Books
ISBN 0 435 00097 7

CHAPTER 1

'GOT YOU!' MILDA miaowed in delight.

But before the kitten could trap the little white chicken feather in her tiny outstretched paws, the breeze blew it away.

Milda was determined not to give up. She chased the feather across yet another field until a strong puff of wind lifted it high up into the air and it floated off over the hedge and out of sight.

Now Milda did give up. She turned back, expecting to find her brother and sisters. All four had chased the feather out of the farmyard. Now they were nowhere to be seen.

Milda tried several promising hiding places, but there was neither sign nor scent of them.

As she looked around the strange field, Milda realised what her mother, Zita, had so often warned her about. She was lost.

Before they were born, their mother had prepared a secret nest in the rich, warm hay, high up near the roof of the old barn. When the kittens arrived, three of them were happy to stay in the nest, cuddled up close to their mother's warm, furry body. Milda, the fourth, was forever tumbling out and wandering away. Zita, gently using her teeth on the scruff of Milda's neck, was constantly lifting her back.

Later, they moved to their second nest, closer to the barn door. Zita did not have so far to carry the kittens' food. Here Milda's habit of roaming off grew worse.

'One day,' Zita warned her, 'you'll wander so far away, nobody will be able to find you. There are things out there more dangerous than you know!'

Now Milda sat alone in the field, feeling very sorry for herself. She wondered if her mother was out looking for her. But perhaps, with so many kittens to feed, she hadn't even noticed one was missing.

The thought of food produced twinges in Milda's stomach. The kittens were old enough to eat solid food, but they still relied on Zita to bring them tasty morsels from her bowl, or things she'd caught around the yard.

Once she had brought them a live mouse so that they could practise pouncing and chasing. But the kittens had become so excited, a fight had developed. The mouse would have escaped if Zita hadn't caught it again.

The sun was getting low in the sky. This was when Zita usually fed her family. Milda wished she was safely back home with the others.

Milda knew night followed once they had been fed. Although she could see well, she was frightened. This would be the first time she had ever been out alone in the dark.

Milda stalked round the field,

staying close to the hedge. She sniffed the air and the tips of plants searching for her own scent. But, although she found slight traces of herself, they proved impossible to follow because so many other animals had criss-crossed her path.

A shower of rain made matters worse. Some smells were washed away, while others, such as nettle and dogs, became stronger than ever.

Milda used her whiskers to measure gaps in the hedge. But each time she squeezed herself through, she found another strange field.

CHAPTER 2

SOON THE SUN had slipped away
behind the hill. Milda felt very lonely
as she crouched down in the deep
grass. She sat listening to all the
strange sounds, trying to remember
what her mother had said they were.

She recognised the distant bark of a
vixen setting off in search of food for
her hungry fox cubs. Much closer was
a noisy, chattering family of fieldmice.

As the last rays of daylight faded in the sky, two barn owls screeched at each other and then flew off into the night.

The owls silently glided across the fields towards the mice, swooping low over Milda. Her whiskers felt the breeze from their wings and she heard it rustle through their feathers.

Milda stumbled across a hedgehog, rolled up in a spiky ball.

She jabbed it with her paw, but the spines hurt the soft pads and she quickly backed away.

Next she came upon a baby rabbit sitting outside its burrow. It was hardly bigger than herself. It was busy nibbling the tips off the dew-laden grass. The meeting surprised Milda as much as the rabbit. They stared blankly at each other. Milda thought the rabbit might prove a tasty meal. If only she could catch it.

Then mother rabbit arrived. Drumming her hind legs on the ground, to warn other rabbits there was a cat about, she collected her baby and disappeared down their burrow.

Milda heard distant human voices. She thought one might belong to the farmer who owned the barn where she lived. She scampered, as fast as possible, across two fields. As she got closer, the smells of the farmyard grew stronger. But when Milda looked across the yard, expecting to see the welcoming gap at the bottom of the old barn door, she got a nasty shock.

Where her stone barn should have been, a new Dutch barn stood, stuffed with bales of sweet-smelling straw.

This wasn't her farm after all!

'Oh, dear!' Milda sighed. 'But at least I can sleep in that warm straw and I might find something to eat here too.'

Her nose twitched hungrily. There was a tempting smell coming from the direction of the farmhouse.

Outside the open back door were two metal bowls. One held some scraps of meat, the other, a few drops of milk. It wasn't much, but Milda was only a small kitten with a tiny stomach.

She was so hungry, she didn't stop to wonder *why* the food had been put outside the door. The meat was in her mouth, its rich taste on her tongue, when there was a loud, warning yowl from the doorway.

Milda looked up into the huge yellow eyes of the biggest black cat she'd ever seen.

She froze and the scrap of meat dropped back into the dish.

The black cat yowled again, even louder. Its huge, bushed-out tail twitched angrily.

Milda crouched, her tail between her legs, to show she meant no threat to the older, bigger cat. She also turned her head away, hoping to avoid the gaze of its eyes. She felt as if they were burning into her.

But that wasn't enough for the black cat. He spat, 'How dare you wander onto my territory and steal *my* food!' His ears flattened on his head as he got ready to pounce.

Milda dreaded being attacked by his great claws but she bravely snatched

back the morsel of food before making a
dash for the wall.

The black cat was too quick for her
and he caught up with her in a single
bound. He gave Milda a clout round the
head with his huge front paw. It made
her ears sing and sent her sprawling

across the yard. She lost the precious scrap of food. By the time she had steadied herself from the blow, the black cat was ready to leap on her again. But the farmer shouted at them.

The instant the black cat turned his head away, Milda jumped over the wall and ran as fast as she could, deep into the undergrowth. She didn't pause for breath until there wasn't the faintest whiff of that farm.

CHAPTER 3

MILDA LAY IN the bottom of the hedge licking her ruffled fur back into place.

Washing herself reminded Milda of all the times her mother had done that for her. Milda licked her paws and used them to wash her face. One ear was bleeding from where the black cat's sharp claws had caught it.

Eventually, miserable and hungry, Milda curled herself into a ball and fell into an uneasy sleep.

Bad hunger pangs and the birds' noisy dawn chorus woke Milda early.

Along the hedge, two crows were arguing with each other. Beside them, in the bottom of the ditch, lay a pigeon which had been shot by a farmer.

While the crows continued their quarrel, Milda carefully crept up on the pigeon. Holding it down with her front paws, the way she'd seen her mother do it, Milda used her teeth to tug out some feathers. She spat them out before she eagerly started to eat.

Soon Milda was gorging herself on the delicious meat. She had almost eaten her fill when she suddenly realised it had gone very quiet.

Glancing round, Milda discovered the crows had stopped quarrelling. Their four beady eyes were staring fiercely, straight at her.

Milda left the crows to haggle over the remains of the meal. She slunk through the hedge onto a piece of waste ground, covered in gorse bushes, nettle beds and bramble patches. Milda was bloated by all the food she'd eaten and she found a bank of dry grass, settled herself down in the warm sunshine and fell into a deep, satisfied sleep.

When Milda woke, she stretched lazily, decided she was very thirsty and sniffed the air. On the edge of the waste ground she discovered a small stream.

As her tiny, pink tongue lapped up the refreshing water, Milda thought life here might not be too bad. Of course, the dead pigeon had been a lucky chance and not one which was likely to be

repeated. She would have to find food for herself. But the waste ground seemed to be home for quite a number of shrews, mice and voles.

At that moment, a creature Milda had never seen before appeared from under a stone beside the stream.

It was brown, with two huge, red
eyes, set high on either side of its head.
Its skin was covered in ugly warts and
it used its long back legs to leap along.

'I'm sure I could easily catch that!'

Milda pounced, but the toad jumped
first. She almost caught it with her
second try, but it managed to slither
out from between her paws.

She stalked the toad for ages,
moving carefully through the fringe of
weeds to keep up with it.

When the toad settled to snap up some flies with its sticky tongue, Milda leapt out of the grass and trapped it firmly between her paws.

'Got you this time!' she cried. She sank her needle-sharp teeth into its fat neck.

But the toad's warts held a quick-acting, evil-tasting poison.

Milda leapt off the toad as a searing
pain shot round the inside of her mouth.

Her mouth began to swell, which made her dribble and she was retching so hard, her whole body shook.

While the toad happily hopped away to freedom, Milda ran to the stream. Frantically, she tried to wash away the foul taste.

Later, back on her grassy mound, Milda felt strangely uneasy and restless.

There was something in the air which she didn't recognise. It wasn't a smell, or a breeze. More a kind of *feeling*, which she didn't understand, but which left her unable to settle.

A few moments later, Milda felt the earth tremble slightly through the sensitive pads at the base of her paws.

The sky grew darker and the tremors stronger, until Milda heard a deep, distant rumble.

Without warning torrential rain began to pelt down and Milda dived under a huge gorse bush for shelter.

A sudden, vivid flash of light zipped across the dark sky. It was so bright, it lit up the whole waste patch and made Milda blink. Seconds later, there was another tremendous crash of thunder.

Milda was terrified, but there was nowhere to run from such an enormous monster. Besides, rain was still streaming down and her coat would soon get soaked.

She curled up in a patch of dry leaves and waited patiently for the storm to pass.

That night, when the rain had eased, Milda emerged from her shelter. Cold, wet, hungry and very miserable, Milda found she was marooned on an island.

CHAPTER 4

HEAVY RAIN HAD swollen the stream
into a rushing torrent. It had
overflowed its banks, spread around all
the low ground and left the higher
ground cut off.

Milda hated getting wet. She
bounded from one tiny island to
another and left the waste ground as
quickly as possible.

But where could she go now?

Above the roar of the wind, Milda thought she heard the sounds of humans. She spotted a light in a window. She knew where there were humans there was usually shelter.

Milda made her way towards the light. She fought against the wind which threatened to blow her away like a leaf. She soon became exhausted. Her sodden, mud-stained fur clung to her tiny, shivering body. She hid

behind the cottage to shelter from the bitter wind and let out several loud miaows for help.

The top half of a stable-door opened and a little girl's head looked out. She saw the unhappy kitten crouched down, shivering in the pool of light.

`You poor little thing!' the girl said, and opened the rest of the door.

Milda's first instinct was to run, but she was worn out. She allowed herself to be picked up in the girl's warm, gentle hands and carried inside.

As the door shut, Milda thought, ` Too late for escape now!'

But she needn't have worried. Very gently the little girl wrapped Milda in a towel, while her mother brought a saucer of warm milk.

Milda wished she could explain. What she really wanted was food and water, but she lapped up the milk gratefully.

She had just finished drinking when a noisy man came into the kitchen. He didn't seem at all pleased to see the kitten in their house, but the girl and her mother quickly shooed him away.

The mother found a deep cardboard box. The girl lined it with her old blue woollen cardigan and then lifted the kitten into it.

The girl gently stroked Milda's fur and kept saying something that sounded like, 'Smoky'.

'No,' Milda miaowed, 'my name's Milda.'

But the girl didn't seem to understand. Eventually Milda gave up arguing, snuggled down into the warm bed and fell fast asleep.

CHAPTER 5

´HELLO, SMOKY,´ THE little girl said, the next morning, as she put down another bowl of milk with bits of bread in it. ´I'm sorry we haven't any real cat food.´

Milda, who was starting to understand a little more of what the humans were saying, wolfed the food down. She was climbing back into her comfortable box, when the man insisted she must be put outside.

It was a good thing the wind had dropped and the sun was out, for not long afterwards the three humans left in their car.

Milda spent the morning carefully exploring her new surroundings. She couldn't help thinking about her own family and wondering what they were doing. It would have been so much more fun exploring this new garden with her brother and sisters. She longed to be back with them. She missed Zita dreadfully.

A familiar smell caught Milda's attention. She tracked it down the garden and found a dead mouse which must have been dropped by an owl, flying back to its nest.

She was about to eat it, when she thought of a better idea. One which might sort out her future.

Pleased with herself, Milda spent the rest of the day curled up on top of the coal-bunker, sleeping in the sun.

The noise of the returning car woke her and by the time the little girl had run round the house, Milda was waiting. She stood miaowing by the back door.

'Smoky!' the girl cried, gently sweeping the kitten up in her arms. 'Mummy, she *is* still here! It was lucky we bought that cat food. I *can* keep her now, can't I, Dad? You know how much I've always wanted a cat.'

Before her father could reply, Milda leapt out of the girl's arms, ran towards the shed, poked a paw underneath and dragged out the mouse which she'd hidden there.

For a while Milda pretended to fight with the mouse. Then, carrying it in her teeth, she trotted proudly over to the man and dropped the body neatly between his big feet.

'Oh, look, Dad, she's caught you a mouse! We'll have to keep Smoky if she's a good mouser, won't we, Dad?'

The man grunted something under his breath and stomped off into the

house. Whatever it was, the little girl whispered to the kitten, 'You're mine now, Smoky!'

Milda rubbed herself affectionately against the girl's legs. Though she was slightly puzzled that the girl should be so silly. Surely she knew? Cats always belonged to themselves, not to humans! They may let humans feed them and stroke their fur, but cats always walk alone. If the girl called out, 'Smoky!' (whatever that meant!), she might come, but deep down she would always be Milda.

'But she's a nice girl,' thought Milda. 'I'll teach her about cats, and in exchange, I'll get a good, warm, comfortable home. That seems fair to me!'

And Milda began to purr loudly.